The end of Kate's bed was a lonely place.

Tiger the cat no longer slept there. Tiger died last winter,

so there were only Kate's two feet to keep each other company.

Now Kate woke to full summer with the sun pouring

over the back fence . . .

For Carolyn,
  Rosy, and Sasha

First U.S. paperback edition 2003

The Library of Congress has cataloged the hardcover edition as follows:

Graham, Bob, date.
"Let's get a pup!" said Kate / Bob Graham. — 1st U.S. ed.
p.   cm.
Summary: When Kate and her parents visit
the animal shelter, an adorable puppy charms them,
but it is very hard to leave an older dog behind.
ISBN 978-0-7636-1452-2 (hardcover)
[1. Dogs—Fiction. 2. Dog adoption—Fiction.
3. Pets—Fiction. 4. Animal shelters—Fiction.]
I. Title.
PZ7.G751667 Le 2001
[E]—dc21   00-057208

ISBN 978-0-7636-2193-3 (paperback)

APS 15

15 14 13

Printed in Humen, Dongguan, China

This book was typeset in Bulmer MT.
The illustrations were done in watercolor and ink.

Candlewick Press
99 Dover Street
Somerville, Massachusetts 02144

visit us at www.candlewick.com

CANDLEWICK PRESS

"Let's Get a PUP!" Said Kate

Bob Graham

"Let's get a pup!" said Kate.

"What, a brand-new one?"
said a now wide-awake Mom.
"With the wrapping still on?"
added her breathless dad.
"Pups don't come wrapped,"
replied Kate.
"I know they don't," said Dad.
"It's just a joke."

Mom looked in the paper.

"It must be small," said Kate.

"And cute," said Dad.

"And get all excited," said Kate.

"And run around in circles," said Dad.

"Hmm," said Mom. "LOOK!"

THE RESCUE CENTER
The center for dogs without a home.
The center for dogs all alone.

With their breakfast uneaten,
they dressed and left immediately.

At the Rescue Center they found plenty of dogs
without a home, and lots of dogs all alone. They found . . .

big dogs, small dogs, sniffers and sleepers,
wire-haireds, short-haireds, scratchers, and leapers.

They found fighters and biters, growlers and snarlers, short dogs,
dogs long and thin, and dogs with their cheeks sucked in.

They also found happy dogs, sad dogs,
"take me" dogs, and dogs who couldn't care less.

They saw smelly dogs, fat dogs,
lean and mean dogs, chew-it-up-
and-spit-it-out-at-you dogs,
and dogs like walking nightmares.

Then they saw . . .

Dave.

Dave was so excited
he came out sideways.
He barked twice,
water flew off his tongue,
and he turned a complete
circle in the air.

He was small.
He was cute.
He was brand-new.

Dave climbed right
over the top of Kate,
who briefly
wore him
like a hat.

"He's all that we want," said Kate.

"All that we came for," said Mom.

"We'll take him,"
  said Dad.

Then they saw . . .

Rosy.

And she saw them.

She was old and gray and broad as a table.

It was difficult for her to get to her feet,

but she stood, it seemed, almost politely.

Her eyes watered, her ears went back,

and she radiated Good Intention.

"My wish for you," said Dad,

"is that you could lie on someone's

living-room floor."

"Or on their couch," said Mom.

"Or on someone's bed," said Kate.

Mom's voice shook,

"We would take them all if we could,

but what can we do?"

And with many a backward glance . . .

they slowly walked away.

At home, Dave was everything
that a pup could be,
and more.

On his first night, he cried in his box.

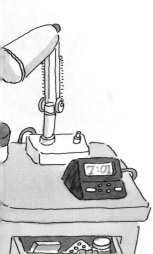

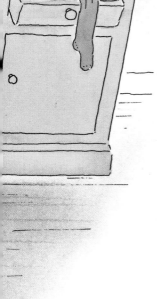

The next morning, Kate's mom and dad
received a good licking.

"Dave was crying last night, so he slept with me,"
said Kate. "But I didn't sleep . . ."

"Neither did I," said Dad. "I was wishing . . ."

"Neither did I," said Mom. "I was wishing . . ."

With their breakfast once again
uneaten, they dressed
and left immediately.

At the Rescue Center
Rosy was waiting for them.

"Let's get you home," said Dad.

Rosy was instantly at home.
Her broad, heavy tail swept everything
off the low table.

"I've seen a dog smelling a man,
   but never a man smelling a dog,"
said Kate's mom.

"She needs a bath," said Dad.

Now Dad's wish has come true.

Rosy is asleep on the living-room floor,

with Dave to keep her company.

Mom's wish has also come true.

Now Rosy and Dave are asleep on the couch.

And what about Kate's wish?

Will it come true as well?

Yes!

Dave and Rosy
will get to sleep
on someone's bed.

Kate puts her head on
Rosy's stomach.
She hears angry gurgles,
squeaks and plops,
lonely corkscrew sounds,
and the pump, pump, pump
of Rosy's heart, like a
big hollow engine room.

Kate's feet are no longer lonely under the blankets.

It seems like Dave and Rosy have always been there.

Their weight is comfortable and reliable, and will stop

Kate's bed from floating away into the night.